# Dr. Welch
## and the
## Great Grape Story

*by* Mary Lou Carney

*Illustrated by* Sherry Meidell

Boyds Mills Press

Text copyright © 2005 by Mary Lou Carney
Illustrations copyright © 2005 by Sherry Meidell
All rights reserved

Published by Boyds Mills Press, Inc.
A Highlights Company
815 Church Street
Honesdale, Pennsylvania 18431
Printed in China

Publisher Cataloging-in-Publication Data  (U.S.)

Carney, Mary Lou.
Dr. Welch and the great grape story / by Mary Lou Carney ;
illustrated by Sherry Meidell.—1st ed.
p. :  ill. ; cm.
ISBN 1-59078-039-6
1. Welch, Thomas Bramwell, 1825-1903 — Juvenile biography.  2. Grape juice — Juvenile
literature.  3. Christian biography — United States — Juvenile literature.  I. Title
[B]  dc22   BR1725.W36C37 2005

First edition, 2005
The text is set in 14-point Clearface Regular.
The illustrations are done in watercolor.

Visit our Web site at www.boydsmillspress.com

*To Amy Jo,*
*our family's*
*great grape juice guzzler*
*—M. L. C.*


*For Grandma Goldie Burt,*
*who loves purple grapes*
*—S. M.*

THOMAS BRAMWELL WELCH had a problem.

It wasn't his wife Lucy,
who filled their house with feathers and lace to make the most beautiful hats.

(She also made terrific apple pies!)

It wasn't his seven children,
George and Fred and Charles Edgar,
Emma and Clara and Villa and May—

who did their chores
and said their prayers and never, ever fought.

(Well, almost never.)

It wasn't the town of Vineland, New Jersey,
where, in this year of our Lord 1869,
the Welches, along with 6,491 other friendly folk,
lived and worked and went to church.

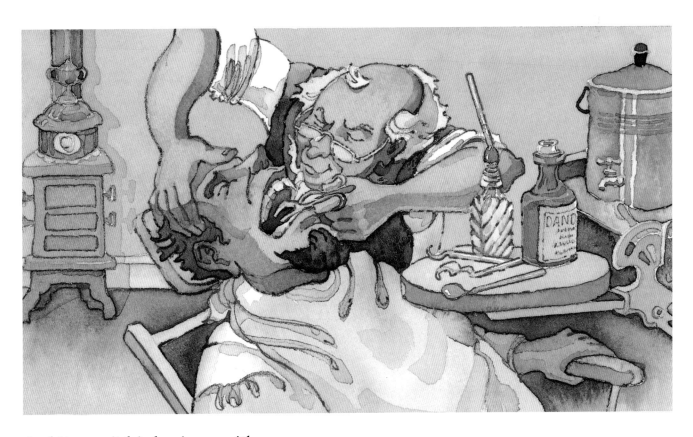

And it wasn't his business, either.
Dr. Welch was a perfectly respectable dentist
with a perfectly respectable office
where he polished and poked and pulled his patients' teeth.
No, Dr. Welch's problem was . . .

# GRAPES.

Specifically,
what people *could* do with grapes…
and what people *couldn't* do with them.

What people could—and did—do with grapes was make wine.
Dr. Welch did NOT like wine.
Not one teeny, tiny bit.
He especially did not like that wine was used in his Methodist church
every time they took communion, the Lord's Supper.

"It just isn't fair," he would say out loud to no one in particular.

"It isn't fair to those poor souls."

Those poor souls were alcoholics,
people so affected by fermented drink
that even one tiny sip—
even communion wine—
could make them crave more and more.

"If only someone could find a way
to use grapes to make a drink that didn't turn into alcohol.
Then the Lord's Supper could be served to everyone.
If only someone…"

And suddenly Dr. Welch realized—
*he* was someone!

Why not invent a new communion drink himself?

But how?
It would, of course, have to be made from grapes.
And everyone knew that grapes, pressed and placed in wooden kegs,
turned into wine. Alcohol.

The fermentation just happened,
naturally,
as part of the process.

"Something to do with yeast, I believe,"
Dr. Welch said, stroking his beard.
What was it he had heard about yeast?
"Ah, yes! That Frenchman!"

That Frenchman was Louis Pasteur.
And what he had discovered was that fermentation happened
because molds and yeast—
both found on grapes—
came together when the grapes were crushed.
And their coming together
was what turned the juice into wine.
Every time.
Pasteur had used this knowledge
to kill off a wild species of yeast
and create a special kind of wine.

Was there another use for this discovery?

The idea of killing off the yeast—all of it—
using Pasteur's method of heating the juice
to hot, hot, temperatures…
no one had ever tried that.

"A drink made from grapes
that does not ferment…ever.
Perhaps *I* could do it!"

It wasn't the first time
Dr. Welch had tried his hand at creating something.
In fact, he *loved* coming up with new ideas.

He had cooked up "Dr. Welch's Neutralizing Syrup" for upset stomachs.

And Dr. Welch's "Sistem of Simplified Spelling" was supposed to
change the dictionary and make spelling tests easier.
(It didn't.)

And his "Phosphate of Zinc" and "Welch's Gold and Platina Alloy"
were popular with dentists all across the country.

So Dr. Welch headed for the grape arbor.

The grapes were big and fat and sweet.

"Come help me, Charles Edgar!" Dr. Welch called to his son.

"We need grapes! Lots of them!"

So they picked and picked (and ate a few) and picked some more.

When their baskets were filled to the brim, they carried them into the kitchen.

"Move over, Lucy! Grapes coming through!"

Dr. Welch filled the counters with pans and funnels, strainers and stew kettles.
Into the pot the grapes went. The fire was lit!
Hotter and hotter and hotter . . . .
Soon the kitchen was filled with the purpleicious smell of grapes.

"Careful, now!" Dr. Welch said as he and Charles Edgar
squeezed the sizzling juice through cloth bags
into four bottles standing on the kitchen table.

*Drip, drip, drip.*
The bottles got fuller and fuller.
*Plunk, plunk, plunk.*
The bottles were sealed with cork and wax.

*Glub, glub, glub.*
The bottles went up to their necks in boiling water.
"Now, we wait," said Dr. Welch, taking out his pocket watch.
"Father," asked Charles Edgar, "what, exactly, are we waiting for?"

Dr. Welch tried to look sure of himself.
"Well, we're waiting for . . . grape juice.
Juice sweet enough for a baby to drink.
Harmless to every soul on God's earth!
The perfect drink for sipping on Sunday—and every other day."

So they waited,
while the boiling water bubbled and gurgled
and the bottles bumped gently into one another.
Finally, Dr. Welch said, "It's time!"

Carefully, one by one,
he and Charles Edgar pulled
the bottles from their hot bath
and placed them on the counter.

"Beautiful!" Dr. Welch pronounced.
And they *were* lovely,
standing in a row like tall soldiers
in purple coats.

But had Dr. Welch done it?
Had he created a new drink made from grapes . . .
or would this juice ferment . . .
and these bottles EXPLODE in a purpleicious mess?

"That could be a big problem," Dr. Welch said.
Lucy nodded her head,
imagining purple stains on her counters, her floor, her ceiling.
"I couldn't agree more!" she said.

"Let us go on with our duties,"
Dr. Welch said, taking one last look at the bottles.
"It is in God's hands now.
Only time will tell."

So, Lucy went back
to making hats.
(And pies.)

And Charles Edgar and his
brothers and sisters went back
to playing in the grape arbor
and (almost) never fighting.

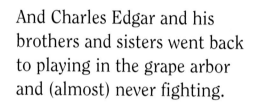

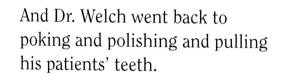

And Dr. Welch went back to
poking and polishing and pulling
his patients' teeth.

And the bottles sat on the kitchen counter,
quietly, day after day.
And do you know what happened?
Nothing.
No broken glass.
No exploding corks.
No fermentation!

But what would this new drink taste like?

Finally, Dr. Welch opened the first bottle
and poured himself a glass of the purple liquid.
After all, he'd been the first to sample Dr. Welch's Neutralizing Syrup.
(And it was not the least bit tasty!)

Sip, sip, sip.
A big smile broke across Dr. Welch's face.
*Success!*
"Lucy!" he said. "Get the children! We have something to celebrate!"

And celebrate they did,
with tall glasses of
pure,
sweet,
grape juice.

Dr. Welch took his second glass
(he had drunk the first one right down!)
out to the grape arbor, and,
surrounded by the smell of his favorite fruit,
he closed his eyes, imagining what communion would be like with his new grape juice.
He pictured the joy of those "poor souls,"
who had lived in fear of taking even a sip of alcohol.
Now they, too, could enjoy the Lord's Supper!

Suddenly, Dr. Welch knew exactly what he had to do next.

Hurrying back into the kitchen, he sat his empty glass on the counter.
"And now," Dr. Welch said, rolling down his sleeves,
slipping on his coat, and placing his hat firmly on his head,
"Now I will take these bottles,
these bottles of GRAPE JUICE,
down to the pastor of our Methodist Church."

And even though the bottles were heavy
and the walk to the church was long,
Dr. Welch found that it really was no problem,
no problem at all.

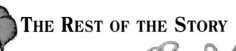

# THE REST OF THE STORY

THE TRIP THOMAS BRAMWELL WELCH'S new-fangled grape juice made from his house to your breakfast table wasn't as quick—or easy—as you might think. While it was true that he had succeeded in producing, as he called it, "Dr. Welch's Unfermented Wine," he could not so easily succeed in making anyone care. To Dr. Welch's great disappointment, the church was not all that interested in his new drink. And, for almost twenty years, most churches kept serving wine for communion.

During the years following his discovery, Dr. Welch tried with all his passion and energy to sell the new drink. He squeezed grapes. He squeezed the family nearly out of their house with his production process. He squeezed himself nearly out of money. He squeezed his friends for help. But in spite of all that squeezing, "Dr. Welch's Unfermented Wine" never took off. And four years after his wonderful success in the family kitchen, Dr. Welch abandoned any plans to sell his new grape juice.

So how *did* this purpleicious drink make it to your breakfast table? For that you can thank Charles Edgar Welch, the son who helped Dr. Welch with that first batch of grape juice. Like his father (and brothers and sisters), Charles Edgar became a dentist. But he could never forget that wonderful day when the juice in his father's experiment had remained nonalcoholic and sweet. So, two years after his father had moved on to other things, Charles Edgar again began trying to make and sell grape juice. And, little by little, orders came in. Soon it was grapes and not teeth that occupied all of Charles Edgar's time. He even convinced his father to help, and in 1897 the two became partners in the Welch Grape Juice Company. Eventually the company moved to Westfield, New York, where there was an abundance of Concord grapes—perfect for making juice. Charles Edgar, a shrewd promoter and manager, succeeded in making grape juice a part of everyday life for thousands of people.

Today, Welch's is the world's leading producer of grape products. Their juices, jellies, and jams are sold in more than thirty countries—with yearly sales totaling $600 million!

And, on any given Sunday, you'll find most Methodist Churches—and lots of other Protestant denominations—serving communion using . . . you guessed it: grape juice.